The Emperor and the Seed

by Katie Dale and Le Nhat Vu

FRANKLIN WATTS
LONDON•SYDNEY

Chapter 1

Long ago in China, there lived a poor boy called Ling.

Ling loved gardening. He grew food to help feed his family, but there was never enough to eat.

One day, Ling was digging in the garden, when

his father ran over.

"Look, Ling," he said, showing him a notice.

"The Emperor is holding a contest!"

"The Emperor is old and has no children," Ling's father told him. "So whoever wins the contest will be the next Emperor. All you have to do is plant a special seed. And you are the best gardener I know."

Ling smiled. "If I become the next Emperor, my family will always have enough to eat," he thought to himself.

Chapter 2

Ling's father took him to the palace to collect his seed. Ling gazed in wonder at the golden rooftops and enormous stone lions. He had never seen such a grand place, nor so many children. The courtyard was filled with thousands of children from all over China.

Suddenly there was a blast of trumpets.

The Emperor had arrived.

"Welcome," the Emperor said. "Every child

will be given one seed. Plant it. Look after it well.

Then, in six months' time, bring it back to me.

Whoever grows the best plant will be

the next Emperor. Good luck."

Ling took his seed home. He planted it in a special pot. He added the best soil from his garden, and looked after it every day. He watered it well, and made sure it was not too hot or too cold.

One month passed ...

Then two ...

Chapter 3

But nothing grew.

"It must be a seed that grows slowly,"

said Ling's father.

Ling nodded. "I will get it some fresh water

from the river."

On his way to the river, Ling passed some boys
from the village.

"Hello Ling," they called. "Has your seed started
growing?"

"No," said Ling, sadly.

"Ha," said one boy. "Mine has grown
a bright green stem."

"Mine has three leaves already."
said the second boy.

"Mine has grown a beautiful flower,"
said the third. Ling frowned.

Ling collected the water from the river

and took it home.

He replanted his seed in fresh soil in a bigger pot.

Three months passed ...

Then four ...

But still his seed did not grow.

Chapter 4

"Hello Ling," the village boys called

as they passed. "Is your plant growing yet?"

"No," said Ling sadly.

"My plant is tall," said the first boy.

"Mine is covered in leaves," said the second.

"Mine has lots of flowers," said the third.

"What am I doing wrong?" Ling sighed.

He wanted to become the next Emperor to help his hungry family, but he would never win the contest if his seed did not grow.

Ling tried replanting his seed again.

He tried putting it in the sunlight.

He tried putting it in the shade.

He tried putting it inside.

He tried putting it outside.

Five months passed ...

Then six ...

But still Ling's seed did not grow.

"Today's the day," the village boys called

excitedly as they walked past his house. "It is

time to show the Emperor our plants."

Ling looked at their beautiful plants..

Then he looked at his pot and sighed.

"I'm not going to the palace," he said.

"Oh yes you are," said his father.

"But I can't show the Emperor my seed,"

cried Ling. "It hasn't grown at all!"

"You have done your best," his father said gently.

"Even the Emperor can't expect more than that."

Ling picked up his plant pot and walked slowly

to the palace.

Chapter 5

The palace courtyard was filled with thousands of children, all holding beautiful plants of all shapes and sizes.

"Where's your plant, Ling?" one boy called.

"Did you forget it?" another boy laughed.

Ling looked sadly at his empty pot.

But Ling's father squeezed his shoulder. "I am proud of you, my son," he said. "I always will be."

Suddenly there was a blast of trumpets.

The Emperor had arrived.

The Emperor slowly made his way along

the line of children. He looked carefully at

every single plant. Ling was last in line.

"Where is your plant, my child?" the Emperor

asked. "Your pot is empty!"

Ling felt his cheeks grow hot.

"I'm sorry, Your Majesty," he said. "I looked after

the seed every day, I gave it fresh water, and

made sure it was not too hot or too cold. I tried

everything I could think of, but no matter what

I did, it would not grow. I have failed the contest."

"No," the Emperor said, smiling. "You have won!"

Ling looked up, confused. "What do you mean?"

"I don't know where all these other children got their beautiful plants," the Emperor said, looking around. "But they did not grow from the special seeds I gave them. Nothing could grow from my seeds, because they had been cooked!"

Ling gasped. Everyone looked at each other in amazement.

"It was not a test of gardening, but a test of honesty," the Emperor told Ling. "You will be a good and fair ruler." He took Ling's hand and turned to the crowd. "Everybody, please welcome your next Emperor!"

Everyone cheered.

"Welcome to your new home, Ling," the Emperor smiled. "I hope you and your family will be very happy here at the palace."

Ling and his family loved their new home. They had plenty of food and never went hungry again.

And when Ling became Emperor he was wise and fair, and made sure that everyone in China always had enough to eat.

Things to think about

1. How does Ling hear about the Emperor's contest?
2. What does his father do to encourage him?
3. How do the other village boys make Ling feel?
4. How does Ling try to make his plant grow?
5. Can you think of any other stories in which honesty is rewarded? Compare it with this story.

Write it yourself

One of the themes in this story is being honest. Now try to write your own story about a similar theme.

Plan your story before you begin to write it.
Start off with a story map:

- a beginning to introduce the characters and where your story is set (the setting);
- a problem which the main characters will need to fix in the story;
- an ending where the problems are resolved.

Get writing! Try to use interesting noun phrases such as "beautiful plants of all shapes and sizes," to describe your story world and excite your reader.

Notes for parents and carers

Independent reading
This series is designed to provide an opportunity for your child to read independently, for pleasure and enjoyment. These notes are written for you to help your child make the most of this book.

About the book
Ling loves growing plants but his family are poor and he can never grow enough food to eat. When the Emperor declares a seed-growing contest Ling is excited - could he win and become the next Emperor?

Before reading
Ask your child why they have selected this book. Look at the title and blurb together. What do they think it will be about? Do they think they will like it?

During reading
Encourage your child to read independently. If they get stuck on a word, remind them that they can sound it out in syllable chunks. They can also read on in the sentence and think about what would make sense.

After reading
Support comprehension and help your child think about the messages in the book that go beyond the story, using the questions on the page opposite. Give your child a chance to respond to the story, asking:
- Did you enjoy the story and why?
- Who was your favourite character?
- What was your favourite part?
- What did you expect to happen at the end?

Franklin Watts
First published in Great Britain in 2020
by The Watts Publishing Group

Copyright © The Watts Publishing Group 2020
All rights reserved.

Series Editors: Jackie Hamley and Melanie Palmer
Series Advisors: Dr Sue Bodman and Glen Franklin
Series Designers: Cathryn Gilbert and Peter Scoulding

A CIP catalogue record for this book is
available from the British Library.

ISBN 978 1 4451 7250 7 (hbk)
ISBN 978 1 4451 7255 2 (pbk)
ISBN 978 1 4451 7259 0 (library ebook)
ISBN 978 1 4451 8088 5 (ebook)

Printed in China

Franklin Watts
An imprint of
Hachette Children's Group
Part of The Watts Publishing Group
Carmelite House
50 Victoria Embankment
London EC4Y 0DZ

An Hachette UK Company
www.hachette.co.uk

www.franklinwatts.co.uk